ANECDOTES OF GRUMPYELLA AND HER FIVE NAUGHTY ELVES

by Susan Chapple

illustrator David Chapple

Published by New Generation Publishing in 2019

First Edition

ISBN 978-1-78955-602-5

www.newgeneration-publishing.com

New Generation Publishing

ANECDOTES OF GRUMPYELLA AND HER FIVE NAUGHTY ELVES.

Grumpyella is a two hundred year old witch. She is very grumpy and bad tempered. This is because she has five elves living with her who are very naughty most of the time. She was given the elves as a present from her dear friend Father Christmas so she couldn't say no. She muttered to herself all the way home to Witches Cottage, casting spells everywhere so creatures far and wide dived for cover.

😄😄😄😄😆😆🤣🤣😄😄😆😆😆😆😆😆 My elves are called, Agis Dior Eldar, Gael, and Levos. Today they get their first lesson on how to treat their elders and also their first magic class. This should be fun, not, oh I feel a migraine coming on. They are imbeciles and need to be taught some sense, from me ha ha ha he he he, oh God

I must lie down the thought is making me ill and I know I will get horrible thoughts and change them into frogs. Go get me some spiders NOW not tomorrow I feel a spell coming on. Curses and all that's horrible why have I to be tormented like this I'm a goodly soul yes? Where are you?, Grumpyella WILL find you, breakfast NOW elves and an aspirin or two. 😵😵😵😵😵😵😵😵😵😵😵😵😵😵 😰😲😰😲😰😲😰😲😎😎😎😎😎😎😎😎🙄🙄🙄🙄🙄🙄 🙄🙄

...

Oh Romeo Romeo read me thy couplet, DO I HEAR SNIGGERING, I was trying to bring a bit of culture into this pig sty you uneducated ignorant worms, curses and all that's horrible. That's it, Hubble bubble....... no? THEN BREAKFAST AND CRISPY CRISPY or else, Grumpyella is on the warpath. Now scuttle off and do my bidding or grumpyellas going to find you a new home with Maybelle at witches croft and she isn't so kind, thoughtful and loving, smirk, as Grumpyella is so LOOKOUT tra la la la la la la 😋. 😋😋😎😆😍🤪🤣😅😄😁😄😅😄😄😄😄😄😄😄😄😎😄 😍🤪🐱

1 Comment

Me and the elves are going snow boarding down Everest, come along don't dawdle, you know you want to with your dear Grumpyella, smirk smirk. That's it hold on tight, off we go weeeeeeeeeeeee, oh no a ledge now we are flying without my broomstick. Up up and DOWN, oh my God we have reached the bottom in a great heap, get off me you little worms now wasn't that fun, did I hear a swear word then, nothing broken, curses and all that's horrible now we have to hike all the way back up, I should have bought my broomstick with me. We must do that again elves, ELVES where are you curses they are hiding, oh well they will soon appear when we have our tea, they won't miss out on food, tra la la la la😄😆😄😄😆😆🤪🤪😄😄😆😄😄😄😄🙂🙂😊😊

The elves are so excited I'm taking them on a flying trip to see my old friends, yes I do have some, curses and all that's horrible. We are meeting up with Bill the bull, flora and Fred and my Dragon friend ha ha ha he he he. Will I regret being nice and kind, probably growl growl. If it will shut the little monsters up for a while I'm all for it. GET UP NOW, or we will be late, no Grumpyella doesn't need breakfast today, snarl, we will have a tea party later, now come ON and don't squash me on the broom, right we have lift off yeah tra tra la la la la la. 😂😂😂😂😂🤣🤣🤣🤣🤣🤣🤣😂😂😂😂😂😂😂😂 😂😂😂😂

Everything is quiet today so far, I chucked the elves another mangy blanket and gave them some marmalade sandwiches to shut up their wailing, got on my nerves and made my toothless jaw jangle. They have a lot to do today, clear the garden of dead rats, get my cauldron out of the berry, stew today and if they are not careful they will be in it ha ha ha he he he. Let's see what I have to go in the stew, frogs, snails puppy dog tails, cats whiskers, a snake or two, rhinoceros eyeballs and some old potatoes, yum, that should do. Now elves BREAKFAST, now you little pipsqueaks or else, Grumpyella is waiting. 😂😂😂😂😂😂😂😂😂😂😂😂😂😂😂😂😂😂😂😎 😎😎😎😎😎😎

I'm bopping and hopping getting it all on down, come on elves let's do the twist yay. What's wrong with me am I going even more insane I do hope so cause it's so much fun, my cloaks swishing my hats askew, God I must lie down, you too elves, what am I saying, no scuttle off and do some housework lol. What a lovely way to start a day now I must go back to bed and recover ta ta ta 😂😂😂😂😂😂 😂😂

ELVES I screech,

breakfast now and my teeth you lazy little worms, you gormless creatures, grumpyella has spoken so jump to it and crispy crispy crispy or else you will become cat food. oh i do love to cast evil spells on my little helpers who are so naughty. no more holidays for you, grumpyella has been too kind to you and you take advantage of my wonderful nature, curses and all that's horrible, mutter, mutter. you won't fly with me today, my broomstick is being locked in the belfry so hurry up before i get a headache, tra la la la la la

there's a coven meeting tonight at midnight down in church street woods, curses and all that's horrible, i was going to try out my new spells tonight. the elves are going to have to wash my beautiful grey matted locks in daffodils oil and cow dung to make it nice and shiny, once a year is enough don't you think. elves i have a headache come and rub grumpyellas brow with that catnip from the larder now not next week, grumble grumble.then elves teeth and breakfast jump to it you little pip squeaks and grumpyella will take you for a fly later if you're good, curses, oh woe is me i hate meetings, someone always tries to steal my spells, curses, see you later tra la la la la la

HASHTAG, URL screeched Grumpyella as she stomped around the kitchen kicking the cat out of her way. Tis a foreign language she stormed or a new way to make spells and no one can do spells like me she raged. WHAT YOU ALL LOOKING AT she bellowed at her elves as they cowered in the corner, GO AND DO SOME SCRUBBING she yelled at them. I must go and lie down, this new fangled machine has got my nerves jangling, oh woe is me, curses and all that'shorrible. Oh for the simple life back again. 😕😕😕😕😕 😕😕😕😕😕😖😖😕😕😮😮😝😝

Tiptoe through the tulips with me, tra la la la la la, cackle cackle. Oh elves I say sweetly, please come up to Grumpyella now there's good elves. Oh I feel ill can't stand this niceness it really isn't me is it. ELVES GET YOURSELVES UP HERE NOW I screech, there that's better, curses and all that's horrible. Today is the witches annual fete and I have to make something, curses. I know elves soup ha ha ha he he he he. No they would probably taste revolting so it's going to be grumpyellas special, ox eyes burgers with salad of worms and cockroaches yum tra la la la la la, JUMP TO IT YOU USELESS, IDLE MORONS, or else, curses.

I'M HAPPY screeched Grumpyella as she sat on the roof of her cottage. The elves can't get at me up here ha ha ha he he he. The little worms can't fly without me so I'm getting some peace. What's that noise, ELVES WHAT ARE YOU UP TO. Oh curses and all that's horrible, they've got the ladder out, oh well she chuckled gleefully if they come up here I can push them off oh ha ha ha he he he. Come on elves come and see the sunset tra la la la la la.😄😄😄 😂😂😅😅😂😄😄😄

ELVES screeched Grumpyella, GET UP YOU LAZY VARMITS, WE ARE GOING TO DO OUR TEN YEARLY SPRING CLEAN she bellowed. Or rather you are she chuckled gleefully. GET THOSE MATTRESSES UP HERE NOW YOU HORRIBLE LITTLE WORMS and look out for spiders oh ha ha ha ha he he he he, I know how you like them. NOW NOT NEXT WEEK curses and all that's horrible tra la la la la la 😄😄😄😄😆😆😆😂😂😄😄😆. 😆😄😆😄😄😄😂😂😆😆😄😄😄😄😄😄😄😄

Grumpyella tripped along merrily and her five elves tripped along merrily behind her. What a lovely sound they made as they all had little bells tied to their ankles. Grumpyella was taking them to the annual Morris dancers ball, she loved dancing and was looking forward to it as long as the elves behaved. She had searched out her newest gown which was only 50 years old and only had a few tatters. It will have to do moaned Grumpyella, curses and all that's horrible and the elves were all in their best suits. She had to force them all into the yonder stream to wash because they smelled of cow dung, what a performance that was sighed Grumpyella. HERE WEELSE BREAD AND WATER FOR A WEEK she warned. Now off you go and I will see you at midnight and don't be late, tra la la la la la la 😄😄😄😄😆😆😆😂😂😄😄😄😄😄😆😆😆😆😊😊😊😊

Now elves, listen to Grumpyella, you two at this end and you two at that end now you turn the rope see, that's right, keep turning. Then watching for her moment grumpyellas leapt in and started skipping, oh yes, not too fast elves then suddenly she was on her bum. YOU NINCOMPOOPS she squawked, as she got up rubbing her posterior. The fair was at the village for a fete and Grumpyella saw the helter skelter in the distance, COME ALONG ELVES and she raced down the field and up the steps. Weeeeeeeeeeeeeee she shrieked this is fun elveswn the shute like a rocket as all the elves were behind her she shot off the end and landed a few feet away in a cow pat. Overcome with rage she yelled YOU NASTY LITTLE WORMS JUST WAIT TIL I GET YOU HOME curses and all that's horrible, muttering and grumbling she stomped off COME ALONG ELVES YOU HAVE SOME WASHING TO DO. 😤😤😐😐😑😑😶😶😶😒

Grumpyella felt so mellow and laid back that she almost fell into the coal scuttle. What's wrong with me she moaned am I ill. Yes that's it I'm ill, someone has put a niceness spell on me, curses and all that's horr nice!!!! NICE? No I'm not having NICE it will ruin my evil reputation, no sir. ELVES WHAT HAVE YOU DONE TO GRUMPYELLA YOU LITTLE MONSTERS, GET UP HERE NOW. No more spell classes for you I'm the boss, no don't smirk at Grumpyella you pipsqueaks she yelled as she stomped around the kitchen we are going to have obedience classes instead. Mutter mutter, curses and all that's HORRIBLE yes I'm back to normal so look out tra la la la la

HASHTAG, URL screeched Grumpyella as she stomped around the kitchen kicking the cat out of her way. Tis a foreign language she stormed or a new way to make spells and no one can do spells like me she raged. WHAT YOU ALL LOOKING AT she bellowed at her elves as they cowered in the corner, GO AND DO SOME SCRUBBING she yelled at them. I must go and lie down, this new fangled machine has got my nerves jangling, oh woe is me, curses and all that's horrible. Oh for the simple life back a cowered in the corner, GO AND DO SOME SCRUBBING she yelled at them. I must go and lie down, this new fangled machine has got my nerves jangling, oh woe is me, curses and all that's horrible. Oh for the simple life back again. 😑😑😮😮😳😳😳😵😵😧😧😧😧😵😵😮😮😵😵

the steps. Weeeeeeeeeeeeee she shrieked this is fun elves ELVES then she was cannoned down the shute like a rocket as all the elves were behind her she shot off the end and landed a few feet away in a cow pat. Overcome with rage she yelled YOU NASTY LITTLE WORMS JUST WAIT TIL I GET YOU HOME curses and all that's horrible, muttering and grumbling she stomped off COME ALONG ELVES YOU HAVE SOME WASHING TO DO. 😤😤😑😑😑😑 😮😮😵😵😵😨😨😧😧

Here we go gathering nuts o may, nuts o may sang Grumpyella as she galloped around the Maypole. She has been crowned this year's coven May queen and is preening at all the attention. That will put Maybelles nose out of joint for sure she chuckled gleefully, silly witch, she can't tell a spell from a candlestick, tra la la la la. Don't you dare snigger at me elves or next time you can stay home and scrub the floors, curses and all that's horrible. Oh I feel dizzy and sick moaned Grumpyella as she landed on the floor in an inelegant heap. Help me up elves and let's go and have some of my ox eye burgers, yum tra la la la la.😂😂😂😂😆😆🤣🤣😂😂😆😆😆😆😆😆 😆

ELVES Grumpyella screamed, she was so cross her face was red with rage and she was jumping up and down. WHICH ONE OF YOU TOE RAGGED WORMS LEFT A BANANA SKIN ON THE FLOOR WHICH I SLIPPED ON AND FLEW ACROSS THE KITCHEN ON MY BOTTOM, she ranted. Whoever did it is going in the stew she fumed, so OWN UP NOW OR BREAD AND WATER FOR A WEEK.Curses and all that's horrible, no sniggering or else she screeched. Oh my bum hurts curses, now do the housework NOW, grumble grumble 🤛🤜😫😫😫😫🙄🙄🙄🙄😒.

So here I am up with the twittering larks this morning and I have aches and pains all over, curses and all that's horrible. My great age of 200 years is beginning to tell curses oh woe is me. Wait a minute the elves aren't up yet, that is all going to change when I bang two saucepans together in their ear holes oh ha ha ha ha he he he he, the day is looking better already. RISE AND SHINE ELVES YOU GORMLESS LITTLE TWITS BREAKFAST NOW AND CRISPY CRISPY OR ELSE. That's done the trick I can hear them scuttling around tra la la la la la my aches and pains seems to have vanished. 😄😄😄😄😅😅🤣🤣😄😄😄😅😅😅😅

Just had my two cups of percolate from one of them new fangled machines and I'm as high as a kite, I mean my broomstick. Come on broom let's see how fast we can go wheeeeeeeeeeeeeee, by my broomometer it's 200 and rising oh I must slow down I feel sick, curses and all that's horrible. I have to remember I'm not a young witch anymore, curses. That was sort of fun so let's have some more ELVES I screech grumpyellas coming for an inspection of your 5 star hovel so shift your bony little asses up here NOW tra la la la la,la la 😚😚😎😎😍😍😽😽😻😻😻😽

Rats and curses and all that's horrible. I've been trying to sleep above the noise of the elves snoring. They sound like a swarm of angry bumble bees, curses. They already sleep in the cellar, amongst the spiders, smirk smirk, maybe I will have to put them out in the cow shed , oh ha ha ha ha ha he he he he, what a good idea. Oh elves I call sweetly, YOU ARE MOVING OUT, so gather up your rags and get busy. I don't want to hear your grumbling Grumpyella has decided so shift your bony arses tra la la la la la la, sweet dreams for me tonight. 😄😄😅😅😅😅🤣🤣😄😄😅😅😅

Facebook reveal thy secrets fumes Grumpyella. She is very moody today because last night at the witches market a friend, yes she has one, curses, told her how to get pictures to come alive, and she can't do it curses. So she is stomping around in a very black mood and spinning spells in her head. CURSES and all that's horrible, these new fangled machines give her such a headache. ELVES GET ME MY SALVES AND MEDICANTS NOW, oh woe is me that's it you little worms, soothe grumpyellas fevered brow, curses.😷😷😖😖😬😑😶😶🙄😌😴😪😫😩😰😥

Rock a hula rock rock a hula shouts Grumpyella as she dances around her cobwebs filled, cesspit of a kitchen. Come on elves she shrieks, dance with Grumpyella, that's it, wriggle those bony little hips, rock rock, a hula, oh God I must sit down all this exertion has given me the vapours. Wasn't that fun elves, what's that, you WANT to do my breakfast NOW, well isn't that kind. Thank you elves but remember Grumpyella knows where the arsenic is so don't even think about it,, curses and all that's horrible, tra la la la la la 😄😄😄😄😄😄😎😎😎😆😆😆🤣🤣😇😇😇😇😆😆😇😇

Hello all you wonderful creatures out there, grumpyellas happy,yes happy tra la la la la la la, the elves are off on a treasure hunt, let's hope they get lost, oh ha ha ha ha ha he he he, oh my I have to sit down haven't laughed so much in a 100 years. I'm going to have my yearly soak in yonder stream, get rid of cobwebs and twigs and soothe my aching bunions. But if they don't get lost they will be back tonight, curses and all that's horrible, still I have time to pamper my beautiful self tra la la la la la 😄😄😄😄😄😆😆😆🤣🤣😄😄😄😄😄😄😄😄😄😄☺️☺️😊😊😍😍😊😊😊😇😇

Ani mini meni mo which is the first elf to go fumes Grumpyella as she stomps around her cauldron. Curses and all that's horrible, they have sniggered at me too often, curses. On second thoughts if I get rid of the elves who's going to look after me, curses foiled again. Oh there you are you gormless twits BREAKFAST, so scuttle off and Grumpyella will speak to you later curses. Tra la la La la la la la 😄 😄

Well what can I say, my ox eye burgers went down a treat, so I stood there basking in the lime light, soaking up the praise like a sponge. Then what do I hear SNIGGERING somewhere in the background, oh just wait til I get you home elves you are going to rue the day you laughed at Grumpyella, oh yes. ELVES I call sweetly, time to go home, oh yes Thank you wizard Dooley I'm glad you liked them, I must now GET my little treasures home now they are so tired. Mutter, mutter curses and all that's horrible, wait for Grumpyella elves, stop hiding away I can see you, mutter mutter, oh my headache is coming on, curses.😷🤕😐😑😕

ELVES GET UP HERE NOW I screech, today you are going to have a spell lesson, I DON'T WANT TO HEAR YOU'RE SNIVELLING, curses and all that's horrible. Don't you want to be as clever as Grumpyella, and DON'T SNIGGER curses. Now collect me, bats wings, plenty of spiders, smirk smirk, juicy worms and tadpoles and cobwebs, NOW NOT NEXT WEEK, be gone you little pipsqueaks, chop chop tra la la la la la la 😄😄😄😄😆😆😂🤣🤣😄😄 😄😆😆😆😆😆😊😊😊😊😀😀😊😊😀😀😀😇😇

If you go down in the woods today be sure of a big surprise tra la la la la la la, because Grumpyella is there with her elves gathering firewood for her cauldron. I can't use them new fangled ovens she crackles, what is this electric anyway she lights her fires with a spell. Step aside you maggots and worms, WHOOSH there we go, curses and all that's horrible tra la la la la la. ELVES BATH TIME AND DON'T YOU RUN AWAY FROM GRUMPYELLA, you all stink of cow dung, you filthy little pipsqueaks, curses and I will turn you into turnips, to eat ha ha ha ha ha ha😄😄😆😆😎😎😍

We're all going on a summer holiday no more worries for a week or two tra la la la la la la, I have a devious plan up my sleeve, ha ha ha . GET YOUR SWIMMING TRUNKS PACKED NOW ELVES or you won't be flying with Grumpyella. The plan is to creep off when the dozy little twerps are sleeping and fly away back home. Can I do it, curses and all that's horrible, I don't know yet, ELVES I screech, GET YOURSELVES UP HERE NOW, or I will leave without you tra la la la la 😄😄😄😄😆😆🤣🤪😄😄😄😄

Mirror mirror on the wall, don't you lie to Grumpyella now, WAIT I screech let me put my teeth in. WAIT I will put on some of that new fangled lipstick, there that's better, now where was I. Mirr...... curses and all that's horrible, the elves are awake. CAULDRON NOW FROM THE BELFRY, stew today and HURRY UP Grumpyella has a headache, curses, you little brainless twits. My peace has gone, oh woe is me, why did I ever miss them curses. 🤫🤫😐😐😑😑😶😶 😶😶😏😏😒🙄😬😳😳😲😧🤧

Hello all you earthlings out there, this is Grumpyella at her most finest. Curses and all that's horrible tra la la la la la. I have the secret to eternal youth of which I am a shining example, did I hear sniggering then, I shall ignore my elves today. Yes the secret is washing oneself in a fountain which is in witches nook, far away and only accessible by broomstick. Yes I will visit today to wash my beautiful, grey matted hair in it. Stop that sniggering, curses, BREAKFAST ELVES NOW jump to it you little gormless twits.tra la la la la, and no you can't come with its grumpyellas day off from you nincompoops, now do some scrubbing which I will inspect when I return. 😄😄😄😄😆😆🤣🤪😄😄😄😄😄😄😄😄😊😊😊 😊

Well suffering bunions, another day another spell, oh my brain is wonderful. I'm going for a fly today but will wear my cloak it's like winter out there, curses and all that's horrible. I'm in a good mood today, can't have that. ELVES polish my broomstick and run my bath NOW, and yes I will have my best bath oil, my favourite that smells of cats pee and bat wings. Now scuttle off and DO AS YOU'RE TOLD tra la la la la la la 😄😄😄😄😆😆🤣🤪😄😄😄😄 😄😄😄😆😊😊😊😊😏😎

I wandered lonely as a cloud, oh for God's sake Grumpyella you have never been poetic in the whole of your two hundred years so don't start now. Well curses and all that's horrible then, I was trying to bring a bit of culture into my toothless world, grumble grumble. Instead my elves will have a dogs life today, or a frogs or a fish ha ha ha he he he, BREAKFAST you worms and jump to it, curses and spells abound today so look out. 😄😄😄😄😅😅🥴🥴😄😄😄😄😄 😄😄😄😊😊😊😊😸😸

WHAT a horrible day Grumpyella moaned, it's raining cats and dogs, but wait, I'm making stew today so they can go in it oh ha ha ha ha he he he he. Oh elves TIME TO GET UP YOU LAZY LITTLE NUMBSKULLS, GET THE CAULDRON OUT, Grumpyella is cooking today and behave or else you WILL be in it too tra la la la la 😂😂😂😂😂😂🤣

HASHTAG, URL screeched Grumpyella as she stomped around the kitchen kicking the cat out of her way. Tis a foreign language she stormed or a new way to make spells and no one can do spells like me she raged. WHAT YOU ALL LOOKING AT she bellowed at her elves as they cowered in the corner, GO AND DO SOME SCRUBBING she yelled at them. I must go and lie down, this new fangled machine has got my nerves jangling, oh woe is me, curses and all that's horrible. Oh for the simple life back again.😑😑😑😑 😳😳😕😕😥😥😰😱😰😱😨😰😨😰😨😰😰😰

Grumpyella was stomping down the lane in a right old fettle when she heard, 'whither art though going my fair maid, she stopped in her tracks and said wha what, she couldn't believe her ears and slowly turned around to see Maybelle simpering at wizard Dooley. Grumpyella carried on stomping saying silly old fool that wizard is, he just wants a new housekeeper since he turned his last one into a goat, curses and all that's horrible, mutter 😂😂😂😂😂😂🤣🤣😂 😂😂😂😂😂😂😊

Nobody loves me everybody hates me I think I will go and eat worms yum sang Grumpyella as she did the washing up. Wait a minute she thought, I'm the boss around here why am I doing the elves chore. The sneaky, lazy little takes, oh elves she called sweetly, Grumpyella has something to show you ha ha ha ha he he he. As they appeared all bleary eyed Grumpyella took something out of her pocket, a massive rubber spider which she threw at them. She watched with glee as they scattered to the high winds and she fell to the floor doubled over with laughter. THAT WILL TEACH YOU NOT TO DO YOUR CHORES she screeched, curses and all that's horrible, BREAKFAST TRA LA LA LA LA LA 😄😄😄😄😄😄.
😂😂😄😄😄

I'm sat here like a fat Toby jug moaned Grumpyella, all this flying around is not giving me any exercise, curses and all that's horrible. ELVES she screeched, come along we are going on a ten mile hike across yonder moor. Not with sandals on you DIMWITS, get your hiking boots on. NOW NOT NEXT WEEK, CURSES. That's it come along, behind me I'm the boss, this will give you a taste of what walking is really about she chuckles to herself. No I'm not carrying your bags you lazy little tykes. Looks like a storm is brewing with any luck I will lose them in the mist h ha ha ha ha he he he 😄😄😄😄😋✈️😄😄😄😄😄😄😄😄😉😉😊.

Mirror mirror on the wall, don't you lie to Grumpyella now, WAIT I screech let me put my teeth in. WAIT I will put on some of that new fangled lipstick, there that's better, now where was I. Mirr...... curses and all that's horrible, the elves are awake. CAULDRON NOW FROM THE BELFRY, stew today and HURRY UP Grumpyella has a headache, curses, you little brainless twits. My peace has gone, oh woe is me, why did I ever agree to have them.😤😤😐😐😑😑😐😶😶 😶😶😒😒😫😫😟😟😨😰😮😮😬

2 Comments

26

I wandered lonely as a cloud, oh for God's sake Grumpyella you have never been poetic in the whole of your two hundred years so don't start now. Well curses and all that's horrible then, I was trying to bring a bit of culture into my toothless world, grumble grumble. Instead my elves will have a dogs life today, or a frogs or a fish ha ha ha he he he, BREAKFAST you worms and jump to it, curses and spells abound today so look out. 😂😂😂😂😆😆🤣🤣😂😂😆😆 😆😆😆😊😊😊😊😋😋😎

ELVES GET UP HERE NOW I screech, today you are going to have a spell lesson, I DON'T WANT TO HEAR YOUR SNIVELLING, curses and all that's horrible. Don't you want to be as clever as Grumpyella, and DON'T SNIGGER curses. Now collect me, bats wings, plenty of spiders, juicy worms and tadpoles and cobwebs, NOW NOT NEXT WEEK, be gone you little pipsqueaks, chop chop tra la la la la la la 😄😄😄😄😆😆🤣🤣😄😄😄😆😆😆 😆😆😜😜😊😊🤗🤗😊😊😊😝😝

Grumpyella is in a reflective mood as she sits in her creaking rocking chair. I'm so glad that I never had any offspring she thinks, stinky, noisy, bawling brats just like the elves she muses. I am far better off with the 5 of them, they do my bidding willingly and lovingly, don't they?. Oh elves she says sweetly, come and sit with your Grumpyella my dears. WHAT curses and all that's horrible I'm getting too soft, SCRUB THE FLOORS she screeches at them, AND THEN BREAKFAST YOU LAZY OAFS, there that will teach them who's boss, tra la la la la la la 😄😄😄😎😆😆🤣🤣😄

Grumpyella tripped along merrily and her five elves tripped along merrily behind her. What a lovely sound they made as they all had little bells tied to their ankles. Grumpyella was taking them to the annual Morris dancers ball, she loved dancing and was looking forward to it as long as the elves behaved. She had searched out her newest gown which was only 50 years oflective mood as she sits in her creaking rocking chair. I'm so glad that I never had any offspring she thinks, stinky, noisy, bawling brats just like the elves she muses. I am far better off with the 5 of them, they do my bidding willingly and lovingly, don't they?. Oh elves she says sweetly, come and sit with your Grumpyella my dears. WHAT curses and all that's horrible I'm getting too soft, SCRUB THE FLOORS she screeches at them, AND THEN BREAKFAST YOU LAZY OAFS, there that will teach them who's boss, tra la la la la la la 😂😂😂😎😆😆😂😂.
😂😂😂😂😂😂😂😂😊😊😊

2 Comments

ohhhhh the Deptford stage is rolling on over the hill yeha sang Grumpyella as she rounded up her few skinny, flea bitten sheep. Well we ain't going to get many meals out of you lot are we curses and all that's horrible. I know I could do a bit of rustling, Maybelle has the best sheep for miles around, what a good idea she preened. Better still send the elves then if they get caught I won't know them, never seen them before ha ha ha he he he. Oh elves Grumpyella has a little job for you oh ha ha ha ha he he 😂😂😂😂😆😆😂😂😂.
😂😂😂😂😂😂😊😊😊😊

2 Comments

hhhhh ohhhhh the Deptford stage is rolling on over the hill yeha sang Grumpyella as she rounded up her few skinny, flea bitten sheep. Well we ain't going to get many meals out of you lot are we curses and all that's horrible. on't know them, never seen them before ha ha ha he he orm😆😂😂😂😂😂😂

obody loves me everybody hates me I think I will go and eat worms yum sang Grumpyella as she did the washing up. Wait a minute she thought, I'm the boss around here why am I doing the elves chore. The sneaky, lazy little takes, oh elves she called sweetly, Grumpyella has something to show you ha ha ha ha he he he. As they appeared all bleary eyed Grumpyella took something out of her pocket, a massive rubber spider which she threw at them. She watched with glee as they scattered to the high winds and she fell to the floor doubled over with laughter. THAT WILL TEACH YOU NOT TO DO YOUR CHORES she screeched, curses and all that's horrible, BREAKFAST TRA LA LA LA LA LA 😆😆😆😆😆😆😆 😂😂😆😆😆😆😆😆😆😊😊😍😍😎😎😍😍😆😆😂😂

v GET UP ELVES I screech, I know how comfortable you are down in the cellar with your moth eaten blanket, but GET UP NOW or else. BREAKFAST you worms Grumpyella is on the warpath ha Ha ha he he he. Today I'm having my yearly beauty treatment, I hear you sniggering, that's ok because today I'm having my eyebrows tattooed on and my many chins lifted so I will look 100 years younger.Thats it, curses and all that's horrible, crispy crispy crispy you little squirts, NOW get on with it tra la la la la.

1 Comment

Write a comment...

There's a coven meeting tonight at midnight down in church street woods, curses and all that's horrible, I was going to try out my new spells tonight. The elves are going to have to wash my beautiful grey matted locks in daffodils oil and cow dung to make it nice and shiny, once a year is enough don't you think. ELVES I have a headache come and rub grumpyellas brow with that catnip from the larder NOW not next week, grumble grumble.Then elves teeth and breakfast jump to it you little pip squeaks and Grumpyella will take you for a fly later if you're good, curses, oh woe is me I hate meetings, someone always tries to steal my spells, curses, see you later tra la la la la la 🐹🐹🐹🐮🐮🐮🦌🦌🦌🐴🐴🐴🐱🐱🐱🐯🐯 🐶🐯🐶👀👀👀👀🐾🐾🐾
LikeShow More Reaction

CPSIA information can be obtained
at www.ICGtesting.com
Printed in the USA
BVHW022352080919
557777BV00035B/467/P

Published by New Generation Publishing in 2019

Copyright © Susan Chapple 2019

First Edition

ISBN 978-1-78955-602-5

www.newgeneration-publishing.com